On a boat ride along the Thames, Lewis Carroll created and recited an extemporaneous fairy tale for the amusement of the children on the cruise. At the behest of his young friend, Alice Liddell, Carroll transcribed this enchanting tale as *Alice in Wonderland* in 1865 and **Through the Looking-Glass** in 1871. The companion books, among the first serious works directed at children, were immediate and extraordinary successes. They were favorites, too, with critics and adults, who were entertained by Carroll's biting social satire, much of it directed at educators and the ruling class. One of the most fanciful stories ever written, **Through the Looking-Glass** tells the story of Alice as she wanders a fascinating dream world, where nothing is as it seems and where the unexpected is always to be expected. Alice's journey through this strange land, by turns humorous and foreboding, introduces her to a delightful assortment of fantastic characters; much as adult life appears to a child, they are alternately comic and threatening. At first wide-eyed and bewildered, by the story's end Alice has become transformed into a confident, resourceful young woman. **Through the Looking-Glass** is a masterpiece of children's literature, engrossing and intelligent. It has also enthralled generations of adult readers, captivated by Carroll's masterful command of wordplay, rhyme, satire and parody, and his ability to conjure up a wonderful world in which the possibilities are restricted only by the bounds of the imagination.

Through the Looking-Glass
Classics Illustrated, Number 3

Wade Roberts, Editorial Director
Alex Wald, Art Director

PRINTING HISTORY
1st edition published February 1990

For information, address: The Berkley Publishing Group, 200 Madison Avenue, New York, New York 10016.

ISBN 0-425-12022-8

Distributed by Berkley Sales & Marketing, a division of The Berkley Publishing Group, 200 Madison Avenue, New York, New York 10016.

Printed in the United States of America
1 2 3 4 5 6 7 8 9 0

Oh, you wicked little thing! Really, Dinah ought to have taught you better manners!

I was so angry, Kitty, when I saw all your mischief. I nearly opened the window, and put you out in the snow, you mischievous little darling! Now don't interrupt me! I'm going to tell you your faults.

Number one: you squeaked twice while Dinah was washing your face. Now you can't deny it, Kitty: I heard you! Her paw went into your eye? Well, if you'd shut them, it wouldn't have happened. No more excuses. Listen!

Number two: you pulled Snowdrop away by the tail as I put down her saucer of milk! What, you were thirsty? How do you know she wasn't thirsty too?

Number three: you unwound every bit of the worsted while I wasn't looking!

That's three faults, Kitty, and you've not been punished for any of them yet. You know I'm saving up your punishments--

Suppose they saved up all my punishments. What would they do at the end of the year? I should be sent to prison, I suppose.

Or suppose each punishment was to go without dinner: when the day came, I should have to go without fifty dinners at once! Well, I shouldn't mind that much! I'd far better go without them than eat them!

Kitty, can you play chess? Now, don't smile. I'm serious. When we were playing just now, you watched as if you understood. When I said "Check!" you purred!

It was a nice check, Kitty, and might have won, except for that nasty Knight that came wriggling among my pieces. Kitty, let's pretend that you're the Red Queen. If you sat up and folded your arms, you'd look exactly like her. Now do try--

--and if you're not good, I'll put you through into the Looking-Glass House. How would you like that?

Now, I'll tell you my ideas about the Looking-Glass House. First, there's the room where you can see through the glass--that's the same as our drawing room, only the things go the other way.

The books are like our books, only the words go the wrong way: I know that, because I've held one of our books up to the glass, and then they hold up one in the other room.

Now we come to the passage. It's very much like our passage as far as you can see, only it might be quite different on beyond. Oh, if we could only get through into the Looking-Glass House!

Let's pretend there's a way of getting through, somehow. Let's pretend the glass is soft like gauze, so that we can get through! Why... it's turning into mist now...! It'll be easy enough to get through--

h, what fun it'll [b]e, when they [s]ee me through [t]he glass in [h]ere, and they [c]an't get at me!

They don't keep this room so tidy as the other.

Here are the Red King and the Red Queen and there are the White King and the White Queen-- and there are two Castles walking arm in arm--

I don't think they can hear me, and I'm sure they can't see me. I feel as if I was getting invisible--

It is the voice of my child! My precious Lily! My imperial kitten!

Imperial fiddlestick!

What volcano?

New... me... [u]p. Mind you [c]ome up--the [r]egular way-- [d]on't get [d]own up!

Why, you'll be hours getting to the table, at that rate. I'd better help you, hadn't I?

Oh! **Please** don't make such faces. You make me laugh so that I can hardly hold you!

I assure you, my dear, I turned cold to the very ends of my whiskers!

You haven't got any whiskers.

The horror of the moment I shall never, never forget!

You will if you don't make a memorandum of it.

eally must get [a] thinner pencil. [I] can't manage this [o]ne a bit: it writes [all] manner of things [th]at I don't intend--

What manner of things? That's not a memorandum of your feelings!

This is a language I don't know.

"'Twas brillig, and
Did gyre and gi
All mimsy were the
And the mome r

"Beware the Jabber
The jaws that bite,
Beware the Jubjub bi
The frumious Banda

He took his vorpal swo
Long time the manxo
So rested he by the Tum
And stood awhile in th

And, as in uffish thought
The Jabberwock,
Came whiffl
An

Why, it's a Looking-Glass book! If I hold it up to a glass, the words will go the right way.

JABBERWOCKY

'Twas brillig, and the slithy toves
   Did gyre and gimble in the wabe:
All mimsy were the borogoves,
   And the mome raths outgrabe.

"Beware the Jabberwock, my son!
   The jaws that bite, the claws that catc
Beware the Jubjub bird, and shun
   The frumious Bandersnatch!"

He took his vorpal sword in hand:
   Long time the manxome foe he sough
So rested he by the Tumtum tree,
   And stood awhile in thought.

And, as in uffish thought he stood,
   The Jabberwock, with eyes of flame,
Came whiffling through the tulgey wood
   And burbled as it came!

One, two! One, two! And through and
through
   The vorpal blade went snicker-snack!
He left it dead, and with his head
   He went galumphing back.

"And hast thou slain the Jabberwock?
   Come to my arms, my beamish boy!
O frabjous day! Callooh! Callay!"
   He chortled in his joy.

'Twas brillig, and the slithy toves
   Did gyre and gimble in the wabe:
All mimsy were the borogoves,
   And the mome raths outgrabe.

It's very pretty, but hard to understand! It seems to fill my head with ideas--only I don't exactly know what they are! However, somebody killed something: that's clear, at any rate--

But oh! if I don't hurry, I'll have to go back through the Looking-Glass, before I've seen the rest! Let's have a look at the garden first!

O Tiger-Lily! I wish you could talk!

We can talk, when there's anybody worth talking to.

Can all the flowers talk?

As well as you, and a great deal louder.

It's not right for us to begin. I was wondering when you'd speak! Said I to myself, "Her face has got sense in it, though it's not clever!" Still, you're the right color.

Aren't you frightened at being planted out here, with nobody to take care of you?

There's the tree in the middle. What else is it good for?

But what could it do, if any danger came?

It could bark.

It says bough-wough! That's why its branches are called boughs! | Didn't you **know** that? | If you don't hold your tongues I'll pick you! | That's right! The daisies are worst of all. When one speaks, they all do. It's enough to make one wither. | How can you talk so nicely? I've been in gardens before, but none of the flowers could talk. | Put your hand down, and feel the ground-- then you'll know why. | It's very hard, but I don't see what that has to do with it.

In most gardens, they make the beds too soft. The flowers are asleep. | I never thought of that before! | It's my opinion you never think at all. | I never saw anybody that looked stupider. | As if you ever saw anybody! You keep under the leaves, and snore away. You no more know what's going on, than if you were a bud! | Are there any more people in the garden besides me? | There's one other flower in the garden that can move like you---but she's more bushy. | Is she like me? | Well, she has the same awkward she but she's red and her peto are shorter.

They are done up close, like a dahlia, not tumbled about, like yours. | But that's not your fault. You're beginning to fade-- and then one can't help one's petals getting a little untidy. | Does she ever come out here? | I dare say you'll see her soon. | She's coming! I hear her footstep. | She's grown a good deal! | The fresh air does it. I should advise you to walk the other way. | Where do you come from? And where are you going? Speak nicely, and don't twiddle your fingers all the time. | I've lost my way...

I don't know what you mean by **your** way--all the ways here belong to me--but why did you come out here at all? | I only wanted to see what the garden was like, your majesty-- | When you say garden--I've seen gardens, compared with which this would be a wilderness. | --and I thought I'd try and find my way to the top of the hill-- | I could show you hills, in comparison with which you'd call it a valley. | No, I shouldn't. A hill can't be a valley. That would be nonsense-- | If you like, but I've heard nonsense, compared with which that would be as sensible as a dictionary!

t's marked out just like a large chessboard! What fun! I wish I was one of them! I wouldn't mind being a pawn--though of course I should like to be a Queen, best.

That's easy. You can be the White Queen's pawn. You're in the Second Square to begin with: when you get to the Eighth Square you'll be a Queen--

Faster! Faster!

Faster! And don't try to talk!

Faster! Faster!

Are we nearly there?

Nearly there! Why, we passed it ten minutes ago! Faster!

Now! Now! Faster! Faster!

You may rest a little now.

Why, I do believe we've been under this tree the whole time! Everything's just as it was!

Of course it is. What would you have it?

In our country you'd get somewhere else if you ran very fast for a long time, as we've been doing.

A slow country! Here it takes all the running you can do, to keep in the same place. To get somewhere else, you must run at least twice as fast as that!

I'd rather not try, please! I'm quite content to stay here.

I'll just take the measurements... At the end of two yards, I shall give you your directions. At the end of three, I shall repeat them in case you forget. At the end of four, I shall say good-bye. And at the end of five, I shall go!

A pawn goes two squares in its first move, you know. So you'll go very quickly through the Third Square--by railway, I think-- and you'll find yourself in the Fourth Square in no time.

That square belongs to Tweedledum and Tweedledee--theFifth is mostly water--the Sixth belongs to Humpty Dumpty--

--the Seventh Square is all forest--

However, one of the Knights will show you the way--and in the Eighth Square we shall be queens together and it's all feasting and fun!

Speak in French when you can't think of the English--turn out your toes as you walk--and remember who you are! Good-bye.

Tickets, please! Show your ticket, child!

Don't keep him waiting!

I'm afraid I haven't got one. There wasn't a ticket-office where I came from.

Don't make excuses.

She ought to know her way to the ticket-office, even if she doesn't know her alphabet!

She'll have to go back from here as luggage!

Changing engines--

Sounds like a horse--

You might make a joke on that-- something about "horse" and "hoarse."

She must be labeled "Lass, with care," you know--

She must be sent as a message by the telegraph--

She must draw the train herself the rest of the way--

Never mind what they say, my dear, but take a return-ticket every time the train stops.

I shan't! I don't belong to the railway journey at all--I was in a wood just now-- and I wish I could get back there.

You might make a joke or that, something about "you would if you could."

ou are so xious to have oke made, y don't you ke one yourself?

I know you won't hurt me, though I am an insect.

What kind of insect?

What, then you don't--

It's only a brook we have to jump over. However, it will take us into the Fourth Square, that's some comfort!

--then you don't like all insects?

When they can talk. None of them talk, where I come from.

What sort of insects do you rejoice in where you come from?

on't rejoice in sects at all, because m afraid of them-- least the large kinds. t I can tell you their mes.

Of course, they answer to their names?

I never knew them to do it.

What's the use of having names, if they won't answer to them?

No use to them, but it's useful to the people that name them, I suppose. If not, why do things have names at all?

I can't say. In the wood down there, they've got no names--However, go on with your list of insects.

Well, there's the horse-fly.

There's a rocking-horse-fly. It's made of wood, and gets about by swinging from branch to branch.

t Sap s and e sawdust.

And there's the dragon-fly.

There's a snap-dragon-fly. Its body is made of plum pudding, its wings of holly-leaves, and its head is a raisin burning in brandy.

And what does it live on?

Frumenty and mince pie, and it makes its nest on a Christmas box.

Then there's the butter-fly.

I wonder if that's why insects fly into candles--because they want to turn into snap-dragon-flies.

There's a bread-and-butter-fly. Its wings are slices of bread and butter, its body is a crust, and its head is a lump of sugar.

And what does it live on?

Weak tea with cream in it.

9

Supposing it couldn't find any?

Then it would die, of course.

But that must happen very often.

It always happens.

I suppose you don't want to lose your name.

No, indeed.

And yet think how convenient it would be if you could go home without it!

If the governess wanted to call you to lessons she would call out "Come here--" And then she would stop. There wouldn't be any name to call, and then you wouldn't have to go.

That would never do. If she couldn't remember my name, she'd call me "Miss."

Well, if she said "Miss," you'd miss your lessons. That's a joke. I wish you had made it.

Why do you wish I had made it? It's a very bad one.

You shouldn't make jokes if it makes you so unhappy.

This must be the wood where things have no names. I wonder what'll become of my name when I go in? I shouldn't like to lose it--they'd have to give me another.

But the fun would be to find the creature that got my old name! That's just like when people lose dogs --"answers to the name of Dash" --fancy calling everything you meet "Alice," till one of them answered!

At any rate, it's a comfort after being so hot, to get into the--into the--into what? I mean under the--under the--under this, you know! What does this call itself, I wonder?

Then it really has happened! And now, who am I? I will remember, if I can! L-- I know it begins with L!

Here then!

What do you call yourself?

I wish I knew! Nothing, just now.

Think again. That won't do.

Please, would you tell me what you call yourself? I think that might help.

I'll tell you, if you'll come a little further. I can't remember here.

I'm a fawn! And, dear me! You're a human child!

However, I know my name now--Alice. I won't forget it again. And now which of these finger-posts ought I to follow?

I'll settle it. When the road divides and they point different ways.

I do believe they live in the same house! But I can't stay long. I'll just say "How d'ye do?" and ask the way out of the wood. If I could only get to the Eighth Square before it gets dark!

CHAPTER 4: TWEEDLEDUM AND TWEEDLEDEE

If you think we're wax-works you ought to pay, you know. Wax-works weren't made to be looked at for nothing. Nohow!

Contrariwise, if you think we are alive, you ought to speak.

I'm sure I'm very sorry.

Tweedledum and Tweedledee Agreed to have a battle; For Tweedledum said Tweedledee Had spoiled his nice new rattle.

"Just then flew down a monstrous crow, As black as a tar-barrel; Which frightened both the heroes so, They quite forgot their quarrel."

I know what you're thinking but it isn't so, nohow.

Contrariwise, if it was so, it might be; and if it were so, it would be; but as it isn't, it ain't. That's logic.

I was thinking, which is the best way out of this wood? It's getting so dark.

First boy!

Nohow!

Next boy!

You've begun wrong! The first thing in a visit is to say "How d'ye do?" and shake hands!

Four times around is enough for one dance.

I hope you're not tired?

Nohow. And thank you very much for asking.

So much obliged! You like poetry?

Ye-es--some poetry. Would you tell me which road leads out of the wood?

What shall I repeat to her?

"The Walrus and the Carpenter" is the longest.

If it's very
long, would
you please
tell me first
which
road--

"The sun was shining on the sea,
Shining with all his might:
He did his very best to make
The billows smooth and bright--
And this was odd, because it was
The middle of the night.

"The moon was shining sulkily,
Because she thought the sun
Had got no business to be there
After the day was done--
'It's very rude of him,' she said,
'To come and spoil the fun!'

"The sea was wet as wet could be,
The sands were dry as dry.
You could not see a cloud because
No cloud was in the sky:
No birds were flying overhead--
There were no birds to fly.

"The Walrus and the Carpenter
Were walking close at hand:
They wept like anything to see
Such quantities of sand:
'If this were only cleared away,'
They said, 'It would be grand!'

"'If seven maids with seven mops
Swept it for half a year,
Do you suppose,' the Walrus said,
'That they could get it clear?'
'I doubt it,' said the Carpenter,
And shed a bitter tear.

"'O Oysters take a walk with us!'
The Walrus did beseech.
'A pleasant walk, a pleasant talk,
Along the briny beach:
We cannot do with more than four,
To give a hand to each.'

"The eldest Oyster looked at him,
But never a word he said:
The eldest Oyster winked his eye,
And shook his heavy head--
Meaning to say he did not choose
To leave his oyster bed.

"But four young Oysters hurried up,
All eager for the treat:
Their coats were brushed, their faces washed
Their shoes were clean and neat--
And this was odd, because, you know,
They hadn't any feet.

"Four other Oysters followed them,
And yet another four;
And thick and fast they came at last,
And more, and more, and more--
All hopping through the frothy waves,
And scrambling to the shore.

'The Walrus and the Carpenter
Walked on a mile or so,
And then they rested on a rock
Conveniently low:
And all the little Oysters stood
And waited in a row.

"'The time has come,' the Walrus said,
'To talk of many things:
Of shoes--and ships--and sealing wax--
Of cabbages--and kings--
And why the sea is boiling hot--
And whether pigs have wings.'

"'But wait a bit,' the Oysters cried,
'Before we have our chat ;
For some of us are out of breath,
And all of us are fat!'
'No hurry!' said the Carpenter.
They thanked him much for that.

'A loaf of bread,' the Walrus said,
'Is what we chiefly need:
Pepper and vinegar besides
Are very good indeed--
Now, if you're ready, Oysters dear,
We begin to feed.'

"'But not on us!' the Oysters cried,
Turning a little blue.
'After such kindness, that would be
A dismal thing to do!'
'The night is fine,' the Walrus said,
'Do you admire the view?

"'It was so kind of you to come!
And you are very nice!'
The Carpenter said nothing but
'Cut us another slice.
I wish you were not quite so deaf--
I've had to ask you twice!'

"'It seems a shame,' the Walrus said,
'To play them such a trick.
After we brought them out so far,
And made them trot so quick!'
The Carpenter said nothing but
'The butter's spread too thick!'

"'I weep for you,' the Walrus said;
'I deeply sympathize.'
With sobs and tears he sorted out
Those of the largest size,
Holding his pocket handkerchief
Before his streaming eyes.

"'O Oysters,' said the Carpenter,
'You've had a pleasant run!
Shall we be trotting home again?'
But the answer came there none--
And this was scarcely odd, because
They'd eaten every one."

13

I like the Walrus best because he was sorry for the poor oysters. He ate more than the Carpenter, though. He held his handkerchief in front, so that the Carpenter couldn't count how many he took.

Then I like the Carpenter best--if he didn't eat so many as the Walrus. He ate as many as he could get.

Z Z Z Z Z! Well, they were both unpleasant. Are there any lions or tigers about here? It's only the Red King snoring.

Come and look at him! Isn't the a lovely sight? Fit to snore his head off!

He's dreaming. Can you guess what he's dreaming about? Nobody can guess that. Why, about you! And if he left off dreaming, where do you suppose you'd be?

Where I am now, of course. Not you! You'd be nowhere. Why, you're only a sort of thing in his dream!

If that King was to wake you'd be out--bang!-- just like a candle! I shouldn't! Besides, if I'm only a sort of thing in his dream, what are you, I should like to know?

Ditto! Ditto, ditto! Hush! You'll wake him if you make so much no

It's no use talking about waking him, when you're only one of the things in his dream. You know you're not real. I **am** real! You won't make yourself a bit realler by crying.

If I wasn't real, I shouldn't be able to cry. I hope you don't suppose those are real tears?

At any rate, I'd better be getting out of the wood. Do you think it's going to rain? No, I don't think it is. At least--not under here. Nohow.

But it may may rain outside? It may--if it chooses, we have no objection. Contrariwise.

14

Selfish things! Good-night.

Did you see that?

It's only a rattle. Not a rattle-snake, only an old rattle--quite old and broken.

I know it was! - It's spoilt, of course!

You needn't be so angry about an old rattle.

But it isn't old! It's new-- I bought it yesterday-- my nice NEW RATTLE!

Of course you agree to have a battle?

I suppose so. Only she must help us to dress up, you know.

I hope you're a good hand at pinning and tying strings? Every one of these things has got to go on, somehow or another.

You know, it's one of the most serious things that can possibly happen to one in a battle--to get one's head cut off.

15

Do I look very pale? | Well-- yes-- a little. | I'm very brave, generally. Only today I've got a headache. | And I've got a toothache! I'm far worse than you! | Then you'd better not fight today. | We must have a bit of a fight, but I don't care about going on long. What's the time now? | Half-past four. | Let's fight till six, then have dinner. | Very well, and she can watch us--only you'd better not come very close. I generally hit everything I see-- when I get excited.

And I hit everything within reach, whether I can see it or not! | You must hit trees very often, I should think! | I don't suppose there'll be a tree left standing, by the time we've finished! | And all about a rattle! | I shouldn't have minded so much, if it hadn't been a new one. | I wish the monstrous crow would come! | There's only one sword, but you can have the umbrella--it's quite sharp. Only we must begin quick. It's getting dark as it can. | And darker.

What a thick black cloud that is! And how fast it comes! I do believe it's got wings! | It's the crow! | It can never get at me here. But I wish it wouldn't flap its wings so--Oh! Here's somebody's shawl!

I'm very glad I happened to be in the way.

Bread-and-butter, bread-and-butter.

Am I addressing the White Queen?

If you call that a-dressing. It isn't my notion of the thing, at all.

If your Majesty will tell me where to begin, I'll do as well as I can.

But I don't want it done at all! I've been a-dressing myself for the past two hours.

Every single thing is crooked...

May I put your shawl straight for you?

I don't know what's the matter with it! I've pinned it here, I've pinned it there, but there's no pleasing it!

It can't go straight, you know, if you pin it all to one side.

Come, you look better now! But you really should have a lady's maid!

I'm sure! Two pence a week and jam every other day.

I don't want you to hire me--and I don't like jam.

It's very good jam.

Well, I don't want it today, at any rate.

You couldn't have it if you did want it. The rule is jam tomorrow, jam yesterday--but never jam today.

It must come sometimes to "jam today."

No, it can't. It's jam every other day: today isn't any other day, you know.

It's dreadfully confusing.

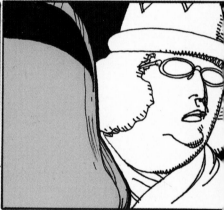

That's the effect of living backwards. It always makes one giddy at first.

Living backwards! I never heard of such a thing!

But there's one great advantage. One's memory works both ways.

Mine only works one way. I can't remember things before they happen.

It's a poor sort of memory that only works backwards.

What sort of things do you remember best?

Oh, the things that happened the week after next. For instance, there's the King's messenger. He's in prison now, being punished: and the trial doesn't even begin until next Wednesday: and of course the crime comes last of all.

Suppose he never commits the crime?

That would be all the better, wouldn't it?

Of course, but not his being punished.

You're wrong, at any rate. Were you ever punished?

Only for faults.

And you were all the better for it!

Yes, but then I had done the things I was punished for. That makes all the difference.

But if you hadn't done them, that would have been better still: better, and better, and better!

There's a mistake somewhere--

Oh, oh, oh My finger is bleeding Oh, oh, oh

hat is e matter? ave you icked ur finger?

I haven't yet, but I soon shall-- oh, oh, oh!

When do you expect to do it?

When I fasten my shawl again. Oh, oh!

You're holding it all crooked!

That accounts for the bleeding. Now you understand the way things happen here.

But why don't you scream now?

I've done all the screaming already. What would be the good of scream-ing again?

The crow must have flown away. I'm so glad. I thought it was night coming on.

wish I could nanage to be glad! ou must be very happy, ving in the wood, nd being glad whenever you like!

Only it is so very lonely here!

Oh, don't go on like that! Consider what a great girl you are! What a long way you've come today! What o'clock it is. Consider anything, only don't cry!

Can you keep from crying by considering things?

That's the way it's done. Nobody can do two things at once. Let's consider your age to begin with--how old are you?

Seven and a half, exactly.

ou needn't say "exactly." can believe it without hat. Now I'll give you omething to believe. I'm ust one hundred and one, ive months and a day.

I can't believe that!

Can't you? Try again: draw a long breath, and shut your eyes.

There's no use. One can't believe impossible things.

I daresay you haven't had much practice. When I was your age, I always did it half an hour a day. Why, sometimes I believed six impossible things before breakfast. I've got it! Now I'll pin it on again, all by myself!

Your finger is better?

Oh, much better! Much be-etter! Be-etter! Be-e-etter! Be-e-ehh!

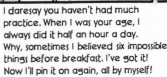

What is it you want to buy?

I don't quite know yet. I should like to look around first, if I might.

You may look in front of you, and on both sides, if you like, but you can't look all around you-- unless you've got eyes in back of your head.

Are you a child or a teetotum? You'll make me giddy soon, if you go on turning round like that.

How can she knit with so many? She gets more like a porcupine every minute!

Can you row?

A little-- but not on land-- and not with needles--

Feather! Feather! You'll be catching a crab directly.

Didn't you hear me say "feather"?

Indeed, you've said it often--ar loud. Please where are the crabs?

In the water, of course! Feather, I say!

Why do you say "feather" so often? I'm not a bird.

You are. You're a little goose.

Oh, please! Scented rushes! Such beauties!

You needn't say "please" to me about 'em. I didn't put 'em there, and I'm not going to take 'em away.

No, I meant-- please, may we pick some? If you don't mind stopping the boat for a minute.

How am I to stop it? If you leave off rowing, it'll stop of itself.

I only hope the boat wouldn't tipple over! Oh, what a lovely one! Only I couldn't quite reach it!

20

The prettiest are always further!

Oh, oh, oh!

That was a nice crab you caught!

Was it? I didn't see it. I wish it hadn't let go-- I should so like a little crab to take home with me!

Are there many crabs here?

Crabs, and all sorts of things. Plenty of choice, only make up your mind. Now, what do you want to buy?

To buy! I should like to buy an egg, please.

Fivepence farthing for one-- twopence for two.

Then two are cheaper than one?

Only you must eat them both, if you buy two.

Then I'll have one, please. They mightn't be at all nice, you know.

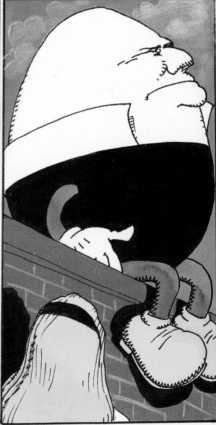

And how exactly like an egg he is!

It's very provoking to be called an egg--very!

I said you **looked** like an egg, Sir. And some eggs are very pretty, you know.

Some people have no more sense than a baby!

"Humpty Dumpty sat on a wall:
Humpty Dumpty had a great fall.
All the king's horses and all the king's men
Couldn't put Humpty Dumpty in his place again."

Don't stand chattering yourself like that. Tell m your name and busine

My name is Alice, but--

It's a stupid name! What does it mean?

Must a name mean something?

Of course. My name means the shape I am-- and a good handsome shape it is, too. With a name like yours, you might be any shape, almost.

Why do you sit here all alone?

Because there nobody with r Did you think I didn't know th answer to that Ask another.

Don't you think you'd be safer on the ground? That wall is so very narrow!

What easy riddles you ask! Of course I don't think so! If I ever did fall off--which there's no chance of--but if I did fall, the **King has promised me**--ah, you may turn pale, if you like! You didn't think I was going to say that did you? The **King has promised me**--to--to--

To send all his horses and all his men.

Now that's too bo You've been lister at doors--and beh trees--and down chimneys--or you wouldn't have kn

I haven't indeed! It's in a book.

Ah, well! They may write such things in a book. That's what you call a History of England, that is. Take a good look at me! I'm one who has spoken to a King, I am: mayhap you'll never see such another: to show you I'm not proud, you may shake hands with me!

If he smiled much more, the ends of his mouth might meet behind. And then I don't know what would happen to his head! I'm afraid it would come off!

Yes, all his horses, and all his men. They'd pick me up again in a minute, they would! But this conversation has gone a little too fast: let's go back to the last remark but one.

I'm afraid I don't remember it.

In that case we start afresh. So here's a question for you. How old did you say you were?

Seven years and six months.

Wrongs! You never said a word like it!

I thought you meant "How old are you?"

If I'd meant that, I'd have said it.

Seven years and six months. An uncomfortable sort of age. Now if you'd asked my advice, I'd have said leave off at seven--but it's too late now.

I never ask advice about growing.

Too proud?

I mean one can't help growing older.

One can't, but two can. With proper assistance, you might have left off at seven.

What a beautiful belt you have on! At least a beautiful cravat, I should have said--no, a belt--I beg your pardon!

It is--most--provoking--when a person doesn't know a cravat from a belt!

I know it's very ignorant of me.

It's a cravat, and a beautiful one. It's a present from the White King and Queen. There now!

Is it really?

They gave it to me--for an un-birthday present.

I beg your pardon?

I'm not offended.

I mean, what's an un-birthday present?

A present when it isn't your birthday.

I like birthday presents best.

You don't know what you're talking about! How many days are there in a year?

Three hundred and sixty-five.

And how many birthdays have you?

One.

And if you take one from three hundred and sixty-five, what remains?

Three hundred and sixty-four, of course.

I'd rather see that done on paper.

That seems about right--

But you're holding it upside down!

To be sure! I thought it looked queer. As I was saying, that seems right--though I haven't time to look it over just now--and that shows that there are three hundred and sixty-four days you might get un-birthday presents--

Certainly.

And only one for birthday presents. There's glory for you!

I don't know what you mean by "glory."

Of course you don't. I meant "there's a nice knock-down argument for you!"

But "glory" doesn't mean he same as "a nice knock-down argument."

When I use a word, it means just what I choose it to mean--neither more nor less.

The question is whether you can make words mean so many different things.

The question is, which is to be master-- that's all. They've a temper, some of them-- particularly verbs: they're the proudest-- adjectives you can do anything with, but not verbs--however, I can manage the whole lot of them! Impenetrability! That's what I say!

Would you tell me, please, what that means?

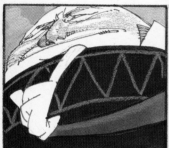   

I meant by "impenetrability" that we've had enough of that subject. It would be just as well if you'd mention what you mean next, as I suppose you don't mean to stop here all the rest of your life.

That's a great deal to make one word mean.

When I make a word do a lot of work like that, I always pay it extra.

Oh! You should see 'em come round to me on Saturday nights to get their wages.

You seem very clever at explaining words, Sir. Would you kindly tell me the meaning of a poem called "Jabberwocky"?

Let's hear it. I can explain all the poems that were ever invented--and a good many that haven been invented yet.

"Twas brillig, and the slithy toves
Did gyre and gimble in the wabe:
All mimsy were the borogoves,
And the mome raths outrcbe."

That's enough to begin with. "Brillig" means four o'clock in the afternoon-- when you begin broiling things for dinner.

And "slithy"?

"Slithy" means "lithe and slimy." "Lithe" is the same as "active." It's like a portmanteau--there are two meanings packed into one word.

And what are "toves"?

"Toves" are something like badgers--they're something like lizards-- and they're something like corkscrews.

  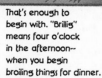  

They must be very curious-looking creatures.

They are that-- also they make their nests under sun-dials--also they live on cheese.

And "gyre" and "gimble"?

To "gyre" is to go round and round like a gyroscope. To "gimble" is to make holes like a gimlet.

And "wabe" is the grass-plot round a sun-dial, I suppose?

It's called a "wabe" because it goes a long way before it, and a long way behind it--

And a long way beyond it on each side.

Exactly. "Mimsy" is "flimsy" and "miserable" (there's portmanteau for you). A "borogove" is a thin shab looking bird with its feath sticking out all round-- something like a mop.

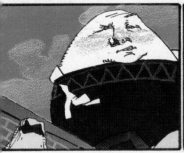
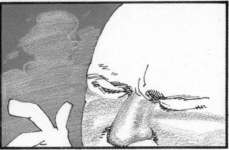

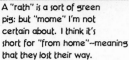nd mome aths"?

A "rath" is a sort of green pig: but "mome" I'm not certain about. I think it's short for "from home"--meaning that they lost their way.

And what does "outgrabe" mean?

"Outgribing" is something between bellowing and whispering, with a kind of sneeze in the middle: you'll hear it done, maybe-- down the wood yonder--and once you've heard it, you'll be quite content. Who's been repeating all this hard stuff to you?

I read it in a book. But I had some poetry repeated to me much easier than that by-- Tweedledee, I think.

As to poetry, I can repeat poetry as well as other folk, if it comes to that--

Oh, it needn't come to that!

The piece I'm going to repeat was written entirely for your amusement.

Thank you.

"In winter, when the fields are white, I sing this song for your delight--" --only I don't sing it.

I see you don't.

If you can see whether I'm singing it or not,, you've got sharper eyes than most.

"In spring, when the woods are getting green, I'll try and tell you what I mean."

Thank you very much.

"In summer, when the days are long, Perhaps you'll understand the song:

"In autumn, when the leaves are brown, Take pen and ink and write it down."

I will, if I can remember it so long.

You needn't go on making remarks like that. They're not sensible, and they put me out.

"I sent a message to a fish: I told them 'This is what I wish.'

"The little fishes of the sea, They sent an answer back to me.

'The little fishes' answer was 'We cannot, Sir, because--'"

I'm afraid I don't
quite understand.

It gets easier further on.
"I sent to them again to say
It will be better to obey.

"The fishes answered, with a grin,
'Why, what a temper you are in!'

"I told them once, I told them twice:
They would not listen to my advice.

"I took a kettle large and new,
Fit for the deed I had to do.

"My heart went hop, my heart went
thump:
I filled the kettle at the pump.

"Then someone came to me and said
'The little fishes are in bed.'

"I said to him, I said it plain,
'Then you must wake them up again.'

"I said it loud and clear:
I WENT AND SHOUTED IN HIS EAR.

"But he was very stiff and proud:
He said, 'You needn't shout so loud!'

"And he was very proud and stiff:
He said, 'I'd go and wake them, if--'

"I took a corkscrew from the shelf,
I went to wake them up myself.

"And when I found the door was locked,
I pulled and pushed and kicked and knocked.

And when I found the door was shut,
I tried the handle, but--"

Is
that
all?

That's all.
Good-bye.

Good-
bye,
till we
meet
again!

I shouldn't know
you again if
we did meet.
You're so
exactly like
other people.

The
face
is what
one
goes by,
generally.

That's just what I complain of. Your face
is the same as everybody's--the two eyes,
so--nose in the middle, mouth under.
Always the same. Now if you had two
eyes on the same side of your nose,
for instance--that would be some help.

It wouldn't
look nice.

Wait
till
you've
tried.

Good-bye.
Of all the
unsatisfactory
people I've
ever met--

C
R
A
S
H

I've sent them all! Did you happen to meet any soldiers, my dear?

Yes, I did. Several thousand, I should think.

Four thousand, two hundred and seven! I couldn't send all the horses, because two of them are wanted in the game. And I haven't sent the two messengers. They're gone to town. Just look along the road, and tell me if you can see either of them.

Nobody.

I only wish I had such eyes. To be able to see nobody! And at that distance too! Why, it's a much as I can do to see real people, by this light!

I see somebody now! But he is coming very slowly--and what curious attitudes he goes into!

Not at all! He's an Anglo-Saxon Messenger--and those are Anglo-Saxon attitudes. He only does them when he's happy. His name is Haigha.

"I love my love with an H because he is Happy. I hate him with an H, because he is Hideous. I fed him with--with--with Ham sandwiches and Hay. His name is Haigha, and he lives--"

He lives on the Hill. The other messenger's called Hatta. I have two, you know--to come and go. One to come, and one to go.

I beg your pardon?

It isn't respectable to beg.

I only meant that I didn't understand. Why one to come and one to go?

Don't I tell you? I must have two--to fetch and carry. One to fetch, and one to carry.

This young lady loves you with an H.

You alarm me! I feel faint--give me a ham sandwich!

Another sandwich!

There's nothing left now.

Hay, then.There's nothing like eating hay when you feel faint.

I should think throwing cold water over you would be better.

I didn't say there was nothing better, I said there was nothing like it.

Who did you pass on the road?

Nobody.

Quite right. This young lady saw him too. So of course Nobody walks slower than you.

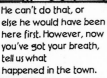

do my best. I'm sure nobody walks much faster than I do!

He can't do that, or else he would have been here first. However, now you've got your breath, tell us what happened in the town.

I'll whisper it. THEY'RE AT IT AGAIN!

Do you call that a whisper? If you do such a thing again I'll have you buttered! It went through my head like an earthquake!

Who are at it again?

Why, the Lion and the Unicorn, of course.

Fighting for the crown?

To be sure. And the best of the joke is, that it's my crown all the while! Let's run and see them!

"The Lion and the Unicorn were fighting for the crown:
The Lion beat the Unicorn all round the town.
Some gave them white bread, some gave them brown: Some gave them plum-cake and drummed them out of town."

Does-- the one-- that wins-- get the crown?

Dear me, no! What an idea!

Would you--be good enough-- to stop a minute?

I'm good enough, only I'm not strong enough. A minute goes by so fearfully quick. You might as well try to stop a Bandersnatch!

He's only out of prison, and he hadn't finished his tea when he was sent in, and they only give them oyster shells in there--so you see he's very hungry and thirsty.

Were you happy in prison, dear child? Speak, can't you!

Speak, won't you! How are they getting on with the fight?

They're getting on very well. Each of them has been down about eighty-seven times.

Then they'll soon bring the white bread and the brown?

It's waiting for 'em now. This is a bit of it I'm eating.

I don't think they'll fight any more today. Go and order the drums to begin.

Look, look! There's the White Queen running across the country! She came flying out of the wood over yonder--how fast those Queens can run!

There's an enemy after her, no doubt. The wood is full of them.

Aren't you going to run and help her?

No use, no use! She runs so fearfully quick. You might as well try to catch a Bandersnatch! But I'll make a memorandum about her if you like-- she's a dear good creature. Do you spell "creature" with a double "e"?

I had the best of it this time?

A little. You shouldn't have run him throughwith your horn, you know.

It didn't hurt him. Who is this?

A child. We only found it today. It's as large as life, and twice as natural!

I always thought they were fabulous monsters! Is it alive?

It can talk.

Talk, child.

always thought Unicorns were fabulous monsters, too. I never saw one alive before!

If you'll believe in me I'll believe in you.

What's this?

You'll never guess! I couldn't.

Are you animal-- vegetable-- or mineral?

It's a fabulous monster!

Then hand round the plum cake, monster. And sit down, both of you.

What a fight we might have for the crown, now!

I should win easy.

I'm not so sure of that.

Why, I beat you all round the town, you chicken!

All round the town? That's a good long way. Did you go by the old bridge, or the market-place? You get the best view by the old bridge.

There was too much dust to see anything. What a time the monster is having!

It's very provoking. I've cut several slices already, but they always join on again!

You don't know how to manage Looking-Glass cakes. Hand it round first, and cut it afterwards.

Now cut it up.

This isn't fair! The monster has given the Lion twice as much as me!

BOOM BOOM BOOM BOOM BOOM BOOM BOOM BOOM BOOM BOOM BOOM BOOM BOOM BOOM BOOM BOOM BOOM BOOM BOOM BOOM

If that doesn't drum them out of town, nothing will!

I wasn't dreaming. Unless we're all a part of the same dream. I only hope it's my dream, and not the Red King's. I've got a mind to wake him...

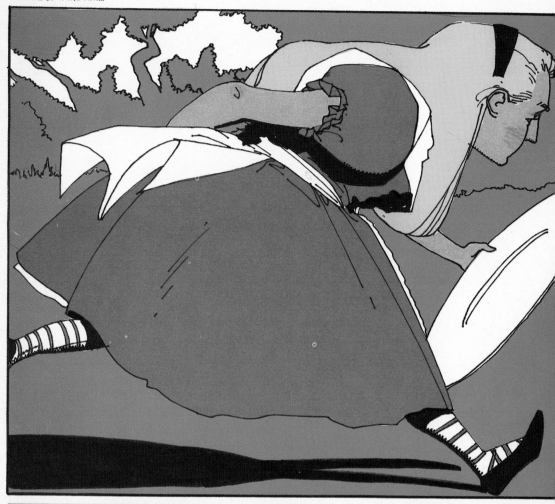

Ahoy! Ahoy! Check! You're my prisoner! You're my--

Ahoy! Ahoy! Check!

She's my prisoner!

But then I came and rescued her!

We must have a fight for her, then.

You will observe he Rules of Battle?

I always do.

It was a glorious victory, wasn't it?

I don't know. I don't want to be a prisoner. I want to be a Queen.

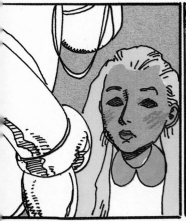

So you will when you've crossed the next brook. I'll see you safe to the end of the wood--and then I must go back. That's the end of my move.

May I help you off with your helmet?

I see you are admiring my little box. It's my own invention-- to keep clothes and sandwiches in. I carry it upside down, so the rain can't get in.

But the things can get out. Do you know the lid's open?

Then all the things must have fallen out! And the box is no use without them! Can you guess why I did that? In hopes some bees may make a nest in it--then I should get the honey.

But you've got a bee-hive-- or something like one-- fastened to the saddle.

It's a very good bee-hive. But not a single bee has come near it yet. The other thing is a mouse trap. I suppose the mice keep the bees out--or the bees keep the mice out. I don't know which.

I was wondering what the mouse trap was for. It's not likely there would be any mice on the horse's back.

But if they do come, I don't choose to have them running all about. It's nice to be prepared for everything. That's why the horse has all those anklets.

But what for?

To guard against the b[ites] of sharks. It's an inventi[on] of my own. And now h[elp] me on. I'll go with you [to] the end of the wood-- What's that dish for?

It's meant for plum-cake.

We'd better take that with us. It'll come in handy if we find any plum-cake. Help me get it into this bag.

I'm afraid you've not had much practice in riding.

What makes you say that?

Because people don't fall off so often, when they've had much practice.

I've had plenty of practice. Plenty of practice. The great art of riding is to keep--

I hope no bones are broken?

None to speak of. The great art of riding, as I was saying, is--to keep your balance properl[y] Like this, you know--

Plenty of practice! Plenty of practice!

It's too ridiculous! You ought to have a wooden horse on wheels!

Does that kind go smoothly?

Much more than a live horse.

How can you go on talking so quietly, head downwards?

What does it matter where my body happens to be? My mind goes on working all the same.

And here I must leave you.

Are you sad? Let me sing you a song to comfort you.

Is it very long?

It's long, but it's very, very beautiful. Everybody that hears me sing it-- either it brings tea[rs] to their eyes, or els[e]

or else it doesn't, you know. The name of the song is called "Haddock's Eyes."

Oh, that's the name of the song, is it?

No, you don't understand. That's what the name is called. The name really is "The Aged Aged Man."

Then I ought to have said "What is the song called?"

No, you oughtn't: that's quite another thing! The song is called "Ways and Means." But that's only what it's called, you know.

Well, what is the song, then?

I was coming to that. The song really is "A-sitting On a Gate." The tune's my invention.

But the tune isn't his own invention, it's "I give thee all, I can no more."

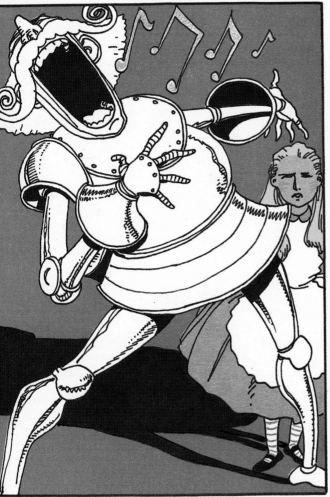

"I give thee everything I can:
There is little to relate.
I saw an aged aged man,
A-sitting on a gate.
'Who are you, aged man?' I said.
'And how is it you live?'
And his answer trickled through my head,
Like water through a sieve.

"He said, 'I look for butterflies
That sleep among the wheat:
I make them into mutton-pies,
And sell them in the street.
I sell them unto men,' he said,
'Who sail on stormy seas;
And that's the way I get my bread--
A trifle, if you please.'

"But I was thinking of a plan
To dye one's whiskers green,
And always use a large fan
That they could not be seen.
So, having no reply to give
To what the old man said,
I cried. 'Come tell me how you live!'
And thumped him on the head.

"His accents mild took up the tale:
He said, 'I go my ways,
And when I find a mountain-rill,
I set it in a blaze;
And hence they make a stuff they call
Rowland's Macassar-Oil--
Yet twopence-halfpenny is all
They give me for my toil.'

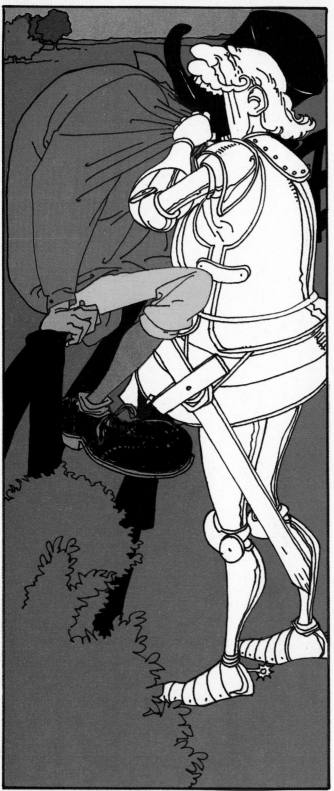

"But I was thinking of a way
To feed oneself on batter,
And so go on from day to day
Getting a little fatter.
I shook him well from side to side,
Until his face was blue:
'Come tell me how you live,' I cried,
'And what it is you do!'

"He said, 'I hunt for haddock's eyes
Among the heather bright,
And work them into waistcoat-buttons
In the silent night.
And these I do not sell for gold
Or coin of silvery shine,
But for a copper halfpenny,
And that will purchase nine.

"'I sometimes dig for buttered rolls,
Or set lined twigs for crabs:
I sometimes search the grassy knolls
For wheels of Hansom-cabs.
And that's the way' (he gave a wink)
'By which I get my wealth--
And very gladly will I drink
Your Honour's noble health.'

"I heard him then, for I had just
Completed my design
To keep the Menai bridge from rust
By boiling it in wine.
I thanked him much for telling me
The way he got his wealth,
But chiefly for his wish that he
Might drink my noble health.

"And now, if e'er by chance I put
My fingers into glue,
Or madly squeeze a right-hand foot
Into a left-hand shoe,
Or if I drop upon my toe
A very heavy weight,
I weep, for it reminds me so
Of that old man I used to know--
Whose look was mild, whose speech was slow,
Whose hair was whiter than the snow,
Whose face was very like a crow,
With eyes, like cinders, all aglow,
Who seemed distracted with his woe,
Who rocked his body to and fro,
And muttered mumblingly and low,
As if his mouth were full of dough,
Who snorted like a buffalo--
That summer evening long ago,
A-sitting on a gate."

You've only a few yards to go-- and then you'll be a Queen. But you'll stay and see me off first? Wait and wave your handkerchief when I get to that turn! It'll encourage me, you see.

Of course I'll wait. And thank you very much for coming so far-- and for the song-- I liked it very much.

I hope so. But you didn't cry so much as I thought you would.

It won't take long to see him off, I expect. There he goes, right on his head as usual!

I hope it encouraged him. And now for the last brook, and to be a Queen! How grand it sounds!

The Eighth Square at last!

Oh, how glad I am to get here! And what's this on my head? But how can it have got there without my knowing it?

Well, this is grand! I never expected I should be a Queen so soon--and I'll tell you what it is, your Majesty. It'll never do for you to be lolling about on the grass like that! Queens have to be dignified, you know! And if I really am a Queen...

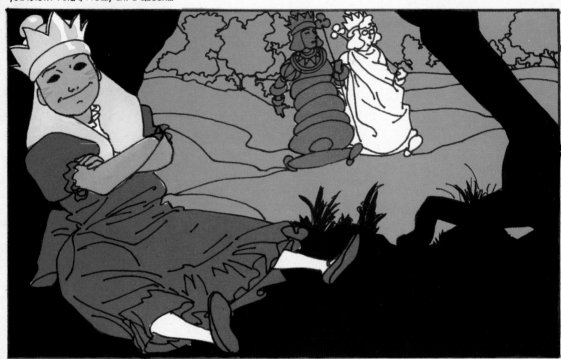

Please, would you tell me--	Speak when you are spoken to!	But if everybody obeyed that rule and if you only spoke when you were spoken to, and the other person always waited for you to begin, nobody would ever say anything, so that--	Ridiculous! What do you mean by "If you really are a Queen?" What right have you to call yourself so? You can't be a Queen, you know, till you've passed the proper examination. And the sooner we begin it, the better.	I only said "if"--	She says she only said "if"--	But she said a great deal more than that Oh, ever so much more than that!

So you did, you know. Always speak the truth--think before you speak--and write it down afterwards.	I'm sure I didn't mean--	That's just what I complain of! You should have meant! What do you suppose is the use of a child without any meaning? Even a joke should have a meaning--and a child's more important than a joke, I hope. You couldn't deny that, even if you tried with both hands!	I don't deny anything with my hands.	Nobody said you did. I said you couldn't if you tried.	She's in that state of mind that she wants to deny something--only she doesn't know what to deny.

A nasty, vicious temper. I invite you to Alice's party this afternoon.

And I invite you.

I didn't know I was to have a party at all. But if there is to be one, I think I ought to invite the guests.

We gave you the opportunity. But I daresay you've not had many lessons in manners yet.

Manners are not taught in lessons. Lessons teach you to do sums, and things of that sort.

Can you do addition? What's one and one and one and one and one and one and one and one?

I don't know. I lost count.

She can't do addition. Can you do subtraction? Take nine from eight.

Nine from eight. I can't, you know, but--

She can't do subtraction. Can you do division? Divide a loaf by a knife--what's the answer to that?

I suppose--

Bread-and-butter, of course. Try another subtraction sum. Take a bone from a dog: what remains?

The bone wouldn't remain, of course, if I took it--and the dog wouldn't remain: it would come to bite me--and I'm sure I shouldn't remain!

Then you think nothing would remain?

Wrong as usual. The dog's temper would remain.

I don't see how.

Why, look here! The dog would lose its temper, wouldn't it?

Then if the dog went away, its temper would remain!

She can't do sums a bit!

Can you answer useful questions? How is bread made?

I know that! You take some flour--

Where do you pick the flower? In the garden or in the hedges?

Well, it isn't picked at all, it's ground--

How many acres of ground? You mustn't leave out so many things.

Fan her head! She'll be feverish from all this thinking!

She's all right again now. Do you know languages? What's French for fiddle-dee-dee?

Fiddle-dee-dee is not English.

What is the cause of lightning?

The cause of lightning is thunder--no, no! I meant the other way.

It's too late to correct it. When you've once said a thing, that fixes it, and you must take the consequences.

I'm so sleepy!

She's a poor thing. Smooth her hair--lend her your nightcap-- and sing her a soothing lullaby.

I haven't got a nightcap with me and I don't know any soothing lullabies.

I must do it myself then.

"Hush-a-by lady, in Alice's lap! Till the feast's ready, we've time for a nap. When the feast's over, we'll go to the ball-- Red Queen, and White Queen, and Alice, and all!"

And now you know the words, just sing it to me. I'm getting sleepy, too.

What am I to do? I don't think anyone ever had to take care of two Queens asleep at once! No, not in the history of England-- it couldn't, you know, because there was never more then one Queen at a time. Do wake up, you heavy things!

I'll ring the--the-- which bell must I ring? I'm not a visitor, I'm not a servant. There ought to be one marked Queen.

No admittance till the week after next!

What is it, now?

Where is the servant whose business it is to answer the door?

Which door?

This door!

To answer the door? What's it been asking of?

What?

It speaks English, doesn't it? Or are you deaf? What did it ask you?

Nothing! I've been knocking at it.

houldn't do that--
houldn't do that--
Vexes it, you know.
You let it alone and
I'll let you alone.

'To the Looking-Glass world it was Alice that said
'I've a sceptre in hand, I've a crown on my head.
Let the Looking-Glass creatures, whatever they be
Come dine with the Red Queen, the White Queen, and me!'

'Then fill up the glasses as quick as you can,
And sprinkle the table with buttons and bran;
Put cats in the coffee, and mice in the tea--
and welcome Queen Alice with
thirty-times-three!'

hirty times
hree makes
ninety!
I wonder
if anyone's
counting?

'''O Looking-Glass creatures,' quoth Alice,
'Draw near!
'Tis an honor to see me, a favor to hear:
'Tis privilege high to have dinner and tea,
Along with the White Queen,
the Red Queen, and me!'

'Then fill up the glasses with treacle and ink,
Or anything else that is pleasant to drink:
Mix sand with the cider, and wool in the wine--
And welcome Queen Alice with
ninety-times-nine!'

Ninety times
nine! Oh,
that'll never
be done!

I'm glad they've come
without waiting to be
asked. I should never
have known who were
the right people to invite!

You've
missed
the soup
and fish.
Put on
the joint!

You look a little
shy: let me
introduce you
to that leg of
mutton. Alice--Mutton:
Mutton--Alice.

It isn't etiquette
to cut anyone
you've been
introduced to.
Remove the joint!

I won't be
introduced to
the pudding,
please, or I
shall get no
dinner at all.

Pudding--
Alice:
Alice--
Pudding.
Remove the
pudding!

Waiter!
Bring
back
the
pudding!

What
impertinence!
I wonder how you
would like it if
I were to cut
a slice out of you!

Make a remark.
It's ridiculous to
leave all the
conversation
to the pudding!

Do you know, I had such a quantity
of poetry repeated to me today,
and it's a very curious thing, I think--
every poem was about fishes in some
way. Do you know why they are
so fond of fishes, all about here?

As to fishes, her
White Majesty knows
a lovely riddle--
all in poetry--
all about fishes.
Shall we repeat it?

Please do.

"First, the fish must be caught."
That is easy: a baby, I think, could have caught it.
"Next, the fish must be bought."
That is easy: a penny, I think, would have bought

"Now cook me the fish!"
That is easy, and will not take more than a minut
"Let it lie in a dish!"
That is easy, because it already is in it.

"Bring it here! Let me sup!"
It is easy to set such a dish on the table.
"Take the dish-cover up!"
Ah, that is so hard that I fear I'm unable!

For it holds like glue--
Holds the lid to the dish, while it lies in the middle
Which is easiest to do,
Un-dish-cover the fish, or dish-cover the riddle?

Take a minute to think about it, and then guess. Meanwhile, we'll drink to your health--Queen Alice's health!

Take care of yourself! Something's going to happen!

Here I am!

I can't stand this any longer!

CHAPTER 10: SHAKING

And as for you--As for you, I'll shake you into a kitten, that I will!

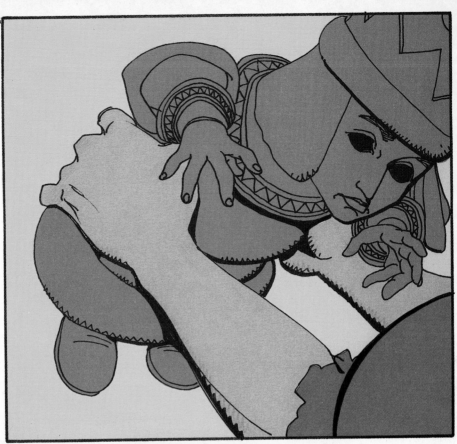

CHAPTER 11: WAKING

And it really was a kitten, after all.

Your Red Majesty shouldn't purr so loud. You woke me out of oh! such a nice dream! And you've been along with me, Kitty--all through the Looking-Glass world. Did you know it?

If only they would purr for "yes," and mew for "no"--so that one could keep up a conversation. But how can you, if they always say the same thing?

Now, Kitty! Confess that was what you turned into! Sit up! And curtsey while you're thinking what to--what to purr. It saves time, remember! Snowdrop, my pet! When will Dinah have finished with your White Majesty? That must be the reason you were so untidy in my dream--Dinah!

Do you know that you are scrubbing a White Queen? Really, it's most disrespectful of you! And what did you turn to? Did you turn to Humpty Dumpty? I think you did--however, you'd better not mention it to your friends just yet.

If only you'd been really with me, there was one thing you would have enjoyed--I had such a quantity of poetry said to me, all about fishes! Tomorrow morning you shall have a real treat

All the time you're eating your breakfast, I'll repeat "The Walrus and the Carpenter" to you; and then you can make believe it's oysters, dear! Now, Kitty, let's consider who it was that dreamed it all. This is a serious question, and you should not go on licking your paw like that--as if Dinah hadn't washed you this morning!

You see, it must have been either me or the Red King. He was part of my dream, of course--but then I was part of his dream, too! Was it the Red King, Kitty? You were his wife, my dear, so you ought to know--Oh, Kitty, do help to settle it! I'm sure your paw can wait!

(WHICH DO YOU THINK IT WAS?)

THE END

LEWIS CARROLL (Charles Dodgson) was born on January 27, 1832, in Daresbury, Cheshire, England, where his father was vicar. Dodgson displayed early literary, artistic and academic interests, producing together with his ten siblings a number of family magazines brimming with parody, acrostics, puzzles and games. Educated at Rugby and Christ Church, Oxford, Dodgson in 1855 won appointment at the latter as a lecturer in mathematics. In 1865, Dodgson, using the pen name Lewis Carroll, published *Alice's Adventures in Wonderland.* Encouraged by the book's success, Dodgson, continuing to write as Lewis Carroll, followed it with *Phantasmagoria* (1869), *Through the Looking-Glass* (1871), and *The Hunting of the Snark* (1876). During this time, Dodgson (using his real name) also invented several educational board games and published a variety of mathematical treatises, such as *Euclid and His Modern Rivals* (1879). While Dodgson and Carroll were widely known to be one and the same, Dodgson shied away from the limelight. In an attempt to protect his privacy, he answered inquiries to Carroll with a strict denial: "Mr. Dodgson neither claimed nor acknowledged any connection with the books not published under his name." After retiring from teaching in 1881, Dodgson served as an elder at Christ Church until his death in 1898. In addition to his fanciful books, Dodgson's legacy includes the perpetual endowment of a bed at a London Children's Hospital.

KYLE BAKER was born in New York in 1965, and studied at the School of Visual Arts. Best known for his work on the highly popular *Shadow* and *Justice, Inc.* series, he wrote and illustrated the graphic novel *Why I Hate Saturn* and the widely acclaimed *The Cowboy Wally Show.* Baker, who once worked for renowned graphic designer Milton Glaser, has also illustrated an adaptation of the Dick Tracy film, and a number of book and magazine covers. Collections of his work have been exhibited by several New York galleries. He would like to thank Valerie Weber for her assistance on this book.